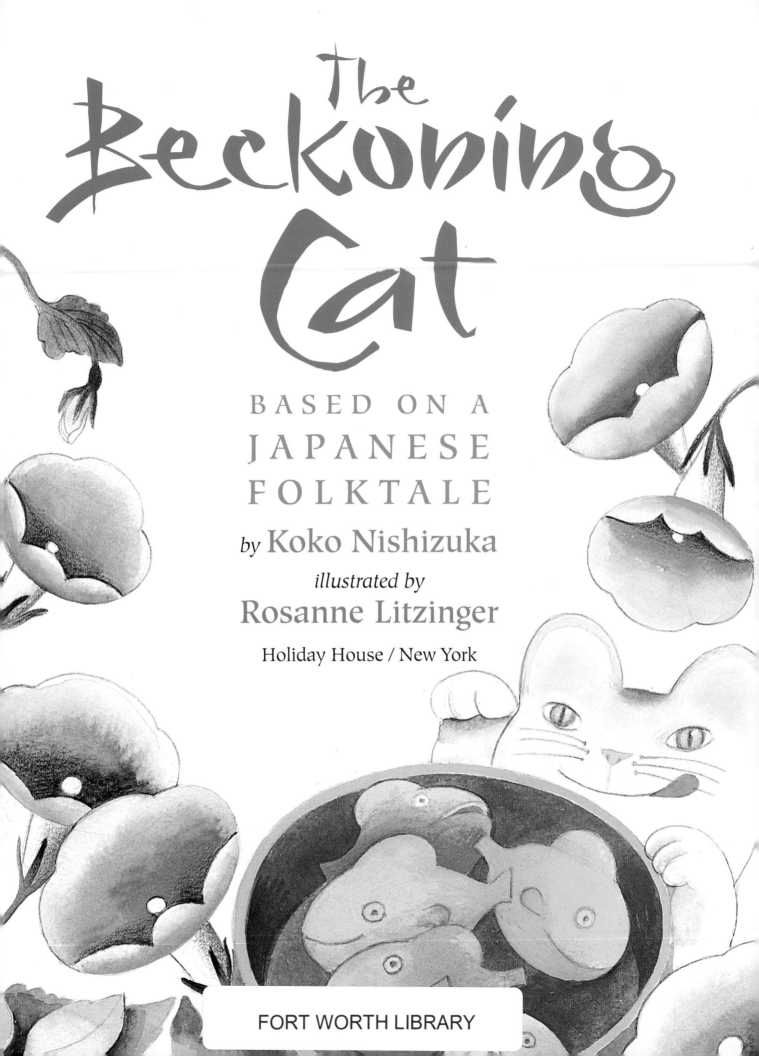

The Beckoning Cat

BASED ON A
JAPANESE
FOLKTALE

by Koko Nishizuka

illustrated by
Rosanne Litzinger

Holiday House / New York

To My Family
K. N.

For Raquel, may good fortune be yours, always.
Love,
R. L.

Text copyright © 2009 by Koko Nishizuka
Illustrations copyright © 2009 by Rosanne Litzinger
All Rights Reserved
Printed and bound in June 2010 at Kwong Fat Offset Printing Co., Ltd.,
Dongguan City, Guan Dong Province, China.
The text typeface is Hiroshige.
The artwork was created with opaque and
transparent watercolors, colored pencil, ink, and gouache
on fine 140-lb. cold-press watercolor paper.
www.holidayhouse.com

3 5 7 9 10 8 6 4 2

Library of Congress Cataloging-in-Publication Data
Nishizuka, Koko.
The beckoning cat : based on a Japanese folktale / by Koko Nishizuka ;
illustrated by Rosanne Litzinger. — 1st ed.
p. cm.
Summary: A retelling of the traditional Japanese tale describing the origins of
the beckoning cat and how it came to be a symbol of good luck.
ISBN 978-0-8234-2051-3 (hardcover : alk. paper)
[1. Folklore—Japan. 2. Cats—Folklore] I. Litzinger, Rosanne, ill. II. Title.
PZ8.1.N61Be 2009
398.2—dc22
[E]
2008007266

LONG, LONG AGO a young boy named Yohei lived
with his father in a village by the sea. Every morning, when the
sun peeked out over the ocean, he got up and went to the port
to buy fish. He then sold the fish door-to-door, carrying them
in two wooden barrels suspended from a pole balanced on his
shoulder. Yohei worked hard, but he was still poor.

When his father became sick, Yohei worked even harder to earn enough money to buy medicine. But he could only carry two barrels of fish at a time. He sighed and wished he could sell more.

One rainy evening, as Yohei was cooking rice at home, he heard a tap on his door. When he opened it, he found a cat shivering in the rain. Her white fur was splattered with mud. She meowed, asking to come in.

"A poor stray cat!" Yohei said as he let her in and dried her with a towel. After serving dinner to his father, Yohei took some rice and half of the fish from his own meager plate and fed the cat.

When she finished eating, the cat jumped into Yohei's lap and rubbed her soft white fur against him. Yohei's stomach growled with hunger, but her purring made him happy. The next morning, the cat was gone.

Three days later, when Yohei was in the village selling fish, his neighbor Masa came running toward him. "Yohei, come home! Your father has a high fever!"

Yohei hurried home, carrying the barrels still heavy with fresh fish. When he arrived, the cat was standing by the door; but Yohei went right to his father. He put a cool damp cloth on his father's forehead. Once his father was comfortable, Yohei looked at the fish and sighed. "What shall I do? I can't go out to sell today, and the fish will spoil by tomorrow."

Suddenly, there was a knock at the door. When Yohei answered, a young woman in a colorful silk kimono stood before him.

"Hello. How can I help you?" Yohei asked in surprise.

"Are you a fishmonger?" she asked, pointing to the fish in the wooden barrels. "How funny, a cat calling a customer to a fishmonger!" She laughed lightly, covering her mouth with her kimono sleeve.

"What do you mean?" Yohei asked.

"Isn't she your cat, the white one? As I left my sewing teacher's home, she meowed at me. After taking a few steps, she turned and waved her paw as if to say, 'Come here.' She was so adorable that I followed her."

Yohei was stunned. He told her how the cat had first visited him. "What a remarkable cat!" the young lady said, smiling. "She must have called me here to buy your fish!" Then she asked him to wrap three fish for her. Bowing, Yohei thanked her.

Soon after, Yohei heard another knock on his door. When he answered, he saw an old man who owned a large store in a nearby town.

"Hello, sir. What brings you here today?" Yohei asked, surprised to see a rich merchant visiting his humble home.

"So, it was *your* cat!" the merchant said, his eyes widening. "She must have heard me talking about fish."

"About fish?" Yohei asked.

"This morning, my daughter-in-law had a baby boy. I wanted ten large red snappers for a party I'm going to give in my grandson's honor. As soon as I left home to look for a fishmonger, your white cat came by and meowed, beckoning me with her paw." He waved his hand, mimicking the cat. "I couldn't help following her. And here you are with all these fish!"

Yohei was so astonished that he told the merchant about his father and how the cat had come to his home.

"My goodness! She's calling customers on your behalf!" said the merchant. "I have never heard of a cat repaying a kindness. These days, even people forget to show their gratitude." Then the merchant took out a silver coin, enough to buy a whole barrel of fish, and gave it to Yohei. "Here is the money for the snappers. Now keep the change and take care of your father."

Yohei thanked the merchant over and over with deep bows.

One after another, people came to Yohei's home, invited by the cat. By the afternoon, the fish in both barrels were gone. The customers praised his cat and promised to come back the next day. In this way, Yohei was able to sell his fish while taking care of his father.

From that day on, the white cat lived with Yohei and kept inviting customers. People came from far away just to see the beckoning cat. Yohei sold more and more fish, and soon he was able to open his own shop. His father got better thanks to the medicine that Yohei was able to buy. All the other merchants wished that they had a cat as clever as Yohei's.

And that is how the beckoning cat became a good-luck symbol in Japan. People began to make porcelain cats holding up one paw like Yohei's cat. Merchants of all kinds put them in their stores in the hopes of bringing in new customers and welcoming old ones.

So, the next time you go to Japan, or even to an Asian restaurant in America, look for the beckoning cat perched on the counter. If she is there, you will know why.